My Two Grandads

My Two Grandads

Floella Benjamin
Illustrated by Margaret Chamberlain

Frances Lincoln
Children's Books

Aston loved music and so did his two grandads.

Grandad Harry, his mum's dad, was from Rochdale in Lancashire, and Grandad Roy, his father's dad, was from the island of Trinidad in the Caribbean. But now both the grandads lived in the same town as Aston and his parents, which made Aston very happy.

And best of all, Grandad Roy and Grandad Harry were musicians.

Aston wanted to be a musician too, and whenever he could, he would find something to play music on. An old biscuit tin to bang on like a drum; a kitchen roll cardboard tube to blow through like a trumpet; two spoons to knock together like castanets, or an empty tissue box with elastic bands round it, to pluck like a guitar.

"I love music," Aston shouted, as he played.

"Yes, we can tell," said his mum and dad, smiling. "You do take after your two grandads!"

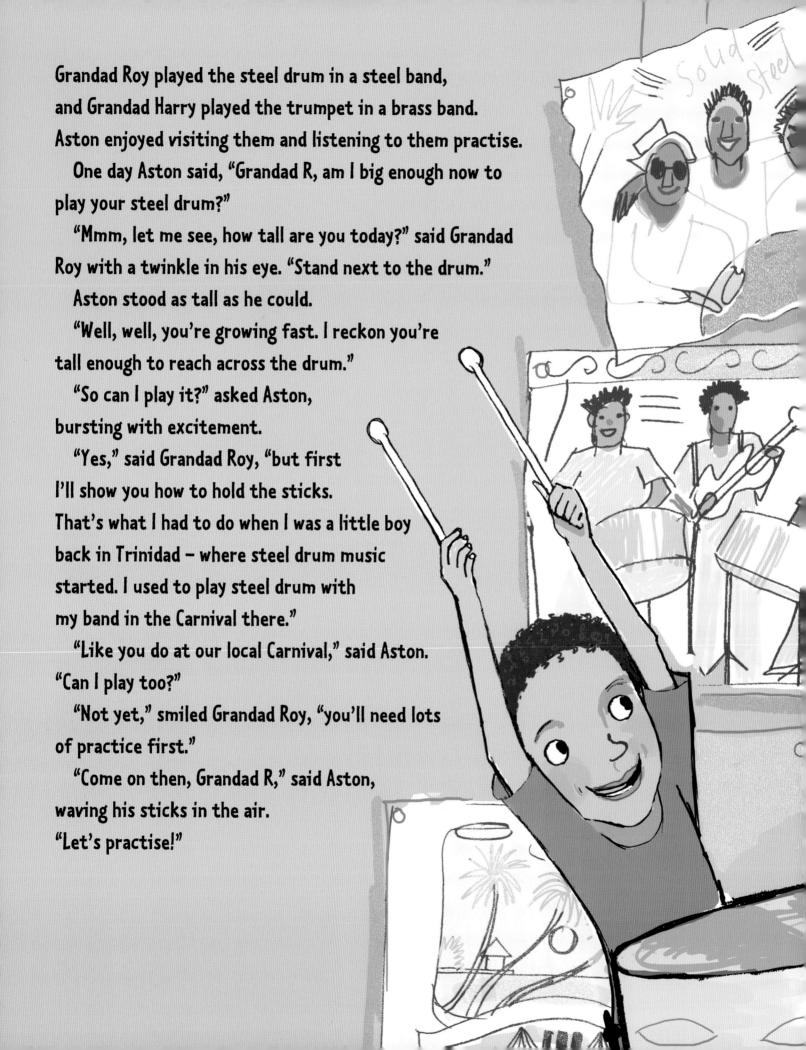

Grandad Roy played the steel drum in a steel band, and Grandad Harry played the trumpet in a brass band. Aston enjoyed visiting them and listening to them practise.

One day Aston said, "Grandad R, am I big enough now to play your steel drum?"

"Mmm, let me see, how tall are you today?" said Grandad Roy with a twinkle in his eye. "Stand next to the drum."

Aston stood as tall as he could.

"Well, well, you're growing fast. I reckon you're tall enough to reach across the drum."

"So can I play it?" asked Aston, bursting with excitement.

"Yes," said Grandad Roy, "but first I'll show you how to hold the sticks. That's what I had to do when I was a little boy back in Trinidad – where steel drum music started. I used to play steel drum with my band in the Carnival there."

"Like you do at our local Carnival," said Aston. "Can I play too?"

"Not yet," smiled Grandad Roy, "you'll need lots of practice first."

"Come on then, Grandad R," said Aston, waving his sticks in the air. "Let's practise!"

Aston loved watching Grandad Harry practise on his trumpet too. It always made him laugh because his grandad's cheeks puffed out while he played, as if they were about to pop!

"Oh, Grandad H, your cheeks always puff out like balloons when you play!"

"That's because I need a lot of air to make a sound come out of the trumpet," laughed Grandad Harry.

"Can I have a go?" asked Aston. "I'd love to learn to play the trumpet."

"Well, you're a big lad now, so I think you'll have enough puff," said Grandad Harry. "Let's see if you can play a note."

Aston put the trumpet to his lips and blew – but no sound came out.

"It's broken, Grandad H."

"No, lad, it's not broken," smiled Grandad Harry. "You have to take a deep breath, squeeze your lips together and blow. Have another go!"

Aston pouted his lips together and blew as hard as he could, but all that came out was a tiny squeak.

"Oh, that sounds funny," laughed Aston.

Grandad Harry laughed too. "Don't worry, lad, it was just the same for me when I started learning to play."

"I wish I could play in a famous brass band like you, Grandad H," said Aston.

"You will one day," said Grandad Harry, "if you practise lots."

"I will," said Aston.

So Aston practised the trumpet whenever he visited Grandad Harry. He puffed out his cheeks and blew as hard as he could, to try to play the notes. He imagined himself playing in Grandad Harry's brass band.

He really enjoyed playing and soon he learnt
his first tune, which went like this...

On Il-kly moor bah t'at   on   Il-kly moor bah

t'at   on   Il   -kly moor bah   t'at

He practised the tune over and over again.

Whenever Aston visited Grandad Roy, he practised on the steel drum. He would sway from side to side and imagine himself playing in the Carnival. Soon he could hit each of the notes marked on the steel drum with the sticks and play a tune, which went like this...

Aston really enjoyed learning to play
the musical instruments with his grandads.

One day at school, Aston's teacher told the class about the Summer Fair. It was being held to raise money for a new school bus.

"Listen, everyone," said Miss Chang. "Will you all please bring in things for the school Summer Fair next Saturday? We need toys, books, food, anything to sell on the stalls."

"We will, Miss," said the children all together.

"There's something else I have to tell you," said Miss Chang sadly. "The band that was coming to play for us at the Fair can't come after all. So it looks like we won't have anyone playing music this year."

Aston and the other children were very sorry to hear this, as they were all looking forward to hearing the band play.

But on his way home from school, Aston suddenly had an idea.
He would ask his grandads if they could help.

When he went to practise the steel drum with Grandad Roy
he said, "My school needs a band to play at the school fair."

"No problem," said Grandad Roy. "My band will play at your
school fair. It will be like a Carnival."

When Aston went to practise the trumpet with Grandad Harry,
he told him about the school fair too.

"Don't worry, lad," said Grandad Harry. "My band will play
at your school fair. It will be fun."

So when Aston went back to school next day, he excitedly told Miss Chang, "I have two bands to play at our Summer Fair."

"That's fantastic, Aston," said Miss Chang, "but I'm afraid we only need one band. There won't be enough time to hear both bands."

'Oh dear,' thought Aston. 'Which band should I choose?'

That evening both grandads came to see Aston, and he told them the sad news that only one band was needed at the school fair.

"Well, that's simple," said Grandad Harry. "My band will play."

"Oh no, you won't," said Grandad Roy. "My steel band will play.
Everyone loves steel band music."

"Everyone loves brass band music too," said Grandad Harry.

"Yes, but the sound of steel band music makes it feel like Carnival time,"
said Grandad Roy. "People can dance to it. We call it jumping up."

"Well, everyone can march along to my brass band music and have
just as much fun, I'll have you know,"
chipped in Grandad Harry.

Aston looked from grandad to grandad as they argued about how much everyone liked their different types of music.

How could he decide which band should play? He loved both his grandads and he didn't want to upset either of them.

Then he had another idea. He jumped up, clapped his hands and shouted, "Grandad R, Grandad H! Why don't the two bands play together? Then everyone will be happy. I enjoy both your kinds of music, and so will everyone else."

The grandads stopped arguing and thought about what Aston had just said. There was a silence as they looked at each other.

The two bands really enjoyed practising and learning each other's music, and soon the sounds of the brass instruments and the tones of the steel drums blended together.

The day of the Summer Fair arrived, and there was a cheer when Aston and the band came on to the stage. Aston was the star of the show. He played first on the trumpet and then on the steel drum. And when the band had finished playing, everyone clapped and cheered.

"Well done, Aston!" said Miss Chang. "You've saved the day. All the grown-ups like the music so much, they've put lots of coins in the collecting bucket for our new school bus."

"That's great," said Aston happily.

"We love playing in your band," said Grandad Harry.

"My band?" exclaimed Aston.

"Well, it was your idea to make one band out of two," said Grandad Roy, "so that makes it your band."

"Thank you, Grandad R, thank you, Grandad H," said
Aston, giving them both a big hug. "I think I'll call
my band The Steel and Brass Musicmakers!"

"Hurray!" shouted the crowd. "Play us another tune."

Aston and his grandads smiled at each other as they struck up the band and played one more time.

"I love playing music," said Aston. "It makes me so happy!" And he gave a big BANG on the steel drum and then a loud TOOT on the trumpet.

To my dad Roy, a dedicated musician who taught me to love music,
and that practice makes perfect. *FB*

For my wonderful, encouraging mother who also wanted me to be a musician. *MC*

Inspiring | Educating | Creating | Entertaining

Brimming with creative inspiration, how-to projects, and useful
information to enrich your everyday life, Quarto Knows is a favourite
destination for those pursuing their interests and passions. Visit our
site and dig deeper with our books into your area of interest:
Quarto Creates, Quarto Cooks, Quarto Homes, Quarto Lives,
Quarto Drives, Quarto Explores, Quarto Gifts, or Quarto Kids.

JANETTA OTTER-BARRY BOOKS

Text copyright © Floella Benjamin 2010
Illustrations copyright © Margaret Chamberlain 2010

First published in Great Britain in 2010 and in the USA in 2011 by
Frances Lincoln Children's Books
First published in paperback in Great Britain in 2019 by
Frances Lincoln Children's Books, an imprint of The Quarto Group.
The Old Brewery, 6 Blundell Street, London N7 9BH, United Kingdom.
T 0)20 7700 6700 F (0)20 7700 8066 www.QuartoKnows.com

A catalogue reference for this book is available from the British Library

ISBN: 978-0-7112-4091-9

Set in Kosmik Three

Manufactured in Shenzhen, China PP012019
1 3 5 7 9 8 6 4 2

MIX
Paper from
responsible sources
FSC® C001701

Have you read the first funny title by Floella Benjamin?

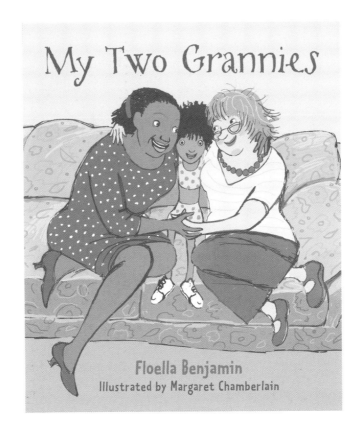

Alvina has two grannies who she loves with all her heart. Grannie Vero is from the Caribbean island of Trinidad. Grannie Rose is from the north of England. When Alvina's parents go away on holiday, both the grannies move in to Alvina's house to look after her. But the two grannies want to do different things, eat different food, play different games and tell different stories. The grannies get crosser and crosser with each other, but Alvina thinks of a way they can do all the things their own way so the grannies can become the best of friends.

ISBN 978-0711240919